The Last Dragon™
W9-AFY-663

The Last Dragon™

Created by Jane Yolen and Rebecca Guay

Story by
Jane Yolen

Art by
Rebecca Guay

Letters by
Clem Robins

Introduction by
Neil Gaiman

Publisher: Mike Richardson

First Edition Editor
Rachel Edidin

Second Edition Editor
Daniel Chabon

Assistant Editors: John Schork, Ian Tucker, and Cardner Clark

Designers: Kat Larson and Justin Couch

Digital Art Technician: Christianne Goudreau

Special thanks to Chris Horn and Rob Simpson

DARK HORSE BOOKS

Published by Dark Horse Books
A division of Dark Horse Comics, Inc.
10956 SE Main Street
Milwaukie, OR 97222

DarkHorse.com

To find a comic shop in your area, call the
Comic Shop Locator Service: (888) 266-4226
International Licensing: (503) 905-2377

First edition: September 2011
ISBN 978-1-59582-798-2

Second edition: April 2016
ISBN 978-1-61655-874-1

1 3 5 7 9 10 8 6 4 2

For Glen, Maddison, Alison, David, and the twins, Caroline and Amelia, who are all magic.

—JY

For Matt and Vivian.

—RG

Introduction

by Neil Gaiman

I met Jane Yolen in October 1988, in London, in a hotel dinner with the late and much-missed Diana Wynne Jones.

I was a former journalist who had just transitioned over to writing comics, as yet mostly unpublished. I couldn't afford to stay in that hotel for the World Fantasy Convention, but Diana had offered me the spare bed in her son's hotel room, and I had gratefully accepted.

I don't know what Jane Yolen thought of me, then. I know only what I thought of her: she was an award-winning writer, eminent and well respected (well respected by me, too—I had read and been impressed by several of her books); she was observant, sharp as tacks, funny as hell. Watching her with Diana was like watching two senior witches, one from each side of the Atlantic, meeting at a witches' convention. (For the record: Diana and Jane took pity on my relative poverty, and they paid for my dinner.)

The next time I ate with Jane Yolen was at a convention in Amherst, Massachusetts. It seems that we were already friends. It was about three years later, and each of the people at that table were or became enormously important to me. (One of them would, two years later, become my assistant for the next twenty years.)

Days blow past like pages falling from an old-fashioned calendar in a black-and-white film, until it was another World Fantasy Convention, this one in Tucson in 1991, and although only three years had gone by, everything had changed, and not just because I could afford a hotel room and pay for my own dinner. That day Charles Vess and I had won the World Fantasy Award, for, of all things, a comic book. We were at a party in the desert, at Terri Windling's house. I told Jane I had started writing a children's book, and I looked up from talking to her and saw a star fall, and the whole of a book that I would call *Stardust* was suddenly in my mind.

I moved with my family to the Midwest. Jane and I stayed friends, and became better friends: I was soon (via my friendship with my assistant Lorraine, who was Jane's daughter-in-law Betsy's best friend) almost an in-law. I got to know Jane better, and as I knew her better I found myself continually awed by her productivity. I preach to young writers the gospel of WRITE! but Jane puts me to shame, and most of the rest of us who write for our lives to shame, because she writes for her life, and for recreation she writes. She writes books for adults and for children, she writes prose and she writes poems. She understood, in a way that so few writers do, that writers write. Whenever I saw her she would be creating something completely different.

Jane was the very first editor to want to publish my children's novel *Coraline*. She read what there was of it, in the early '90s, wanted to publish it in her own line of books, and was hugely disappointed to discover that the publishing company was too scared to allow her to buy it.

And then, one day, Jane told me she wanted to write her first comic, an adaptation of a traditional ballad for Charles Vess's *The Book of Ballads and Sagas*. She must have enjoyed it, because now she has created a short novel in comics form (a graphic novel, if you will, although that could mean so many things).

Rebecca Guay came into my life when she was a young artist, working on Vertigo material in the early '90s. She drew *Black Orchid*, worked on the *Destiny* comic, brought an impressive color and shape sense to her creations: her art and her composition felt classical—her sense of color and of shape reminded me of the formal American and British illustrators whose work I had loved. I enjoyed and admired her work, the painterly sensibility, the intelligence. To my regret, we never worked together directly (she painted a beautiful trading card, of my characters Dream and Death in a longboat, which somehow reminded me both of Arthur Rackham and of N. C. Wyeth, while being obviously her own work).

In *The Last Dragon* Jane and Rebecca work together, on a story of Jane's, to build a story of an island culture, a dragon, a young woman with a head full of herbal knowledge, and a feckless man who learns that it's not enough to look like a hero. It's a story of using your head, and of what true heroes are. Together Jane and Rebecca create a textured culture that feels real, a dragon that isn't even slightly lovable, and people who feel true.

Enjoy it.

Neil Gaiman
Florida

There is a spit of land near the farthest shores of the farthest islands known as Dragonfield. Once dragons dwelt on the isles in great herds, feeding on the dry brush and fueling their flames with the carcasses of small animals and migratory birds.

The dragons slept by the ocean's edge, in the green shade of trees that wept their leaves into the water. The females laid huge clutches of eggs which they buried deep in sand caches between the roots of the trees. Many of the eggs did not hatch, or hatched too early, or much too late.

There are no dragons there now, though the nearer islands are scattered with rocks scored with long furrows, as though giant claws had once been at work. And the land is exceedingly fertile, made so by the flesh and bones of buried behemoths.

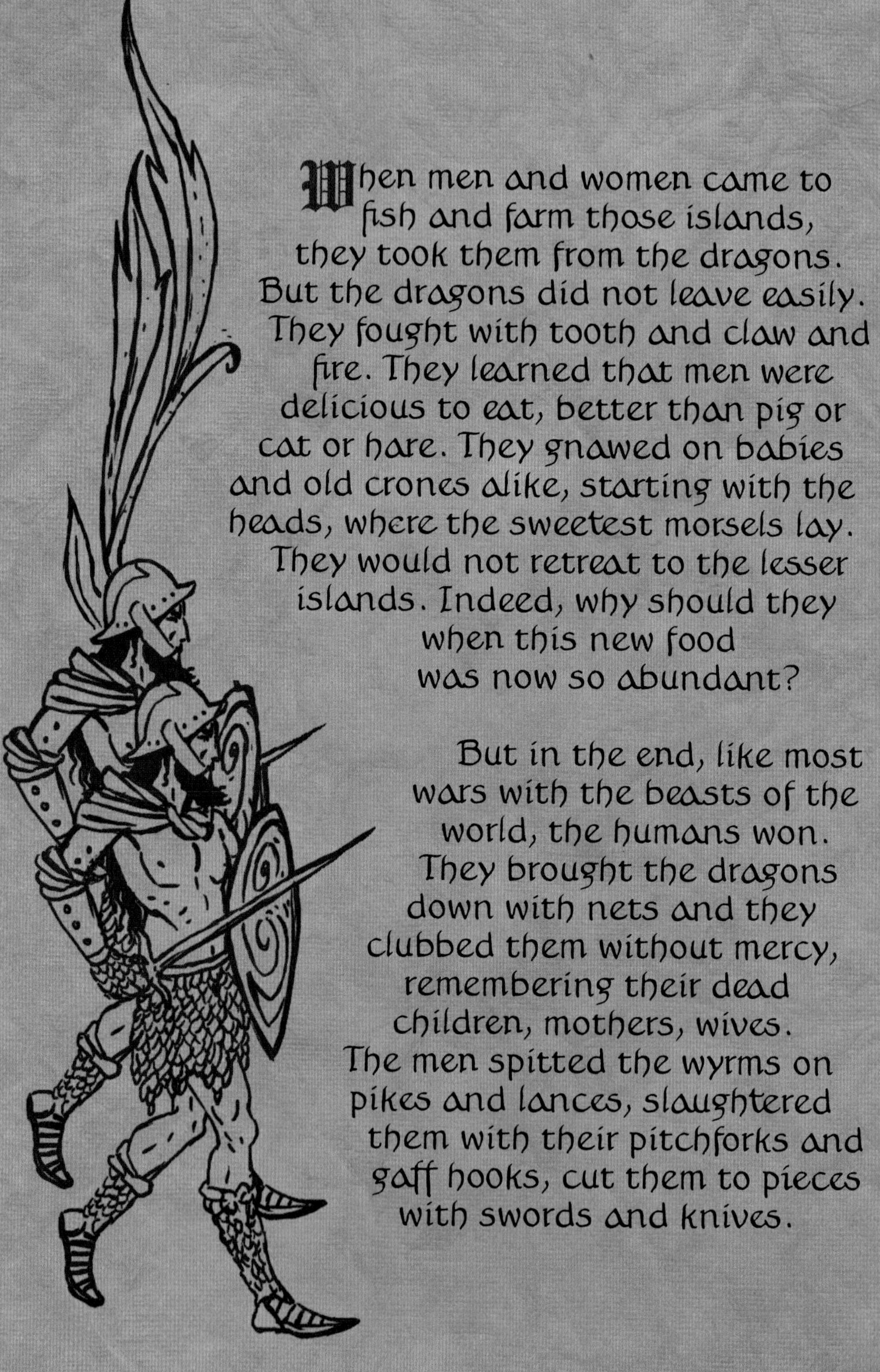

When men and women came to fish and farm those islands, they took them from the dragons. But the dragons did not leave easily. They fought with tooth and claw and fire. They learned that men were delicious to eat, better than pig or cat or hare. They gnawed on babies and old crones alike, starting with the heads, where the sweetest morsels lay. They would not retreat to the lesser islands. Indeed, why should they when this new food was now so abundant?

But in the end, like most wars with the beasts of the world, the humans won. They brought the dragons down with nets and they clubbed them without mercy, remembering their dead children, mothers, wives. The men spitted the wyrms on pikes and lances, slaughtered them with their pitchforks and gaff hooks, cut them to pieces with swords and knives.

The isles
ran red
and dark with
dragon blood
till all of them
were gone.

Or so the
humans
believed.

Two hundred years later.
At sunset the low tide scrapes the beach, pulling cold fingers through the sand and rock.

One great mother tree, older than the long-ago dragons, feels her roots loosening. Slowly, like a mountain, she falls with a crash into the water, giving up her adopted child, the egg she has cradled for so long.
And the story of dragons begins again...

At first the dragon looked like any young lizard, for he had not yet shed his egg-skin, which was lumpy and whitish, like clotted cream. But he grew fast, as dragons will.

Then a family of shagged cormorants on their long migration south. Deer, hare, even a sheep that had wandered away from its flock. He ate them all. After, he soaked in the salty water, to wash off the blood he could not reach with his tongue.

Before the week was out, he was the size of a small pony. His eggskin had sloughed off. He had singed and eaten it, of course, and so developed a taste for crackling.

A small black-snouted island pig was his next meal.

Still no human remarked him. It was the time of the harvests, and everyone was
needed in the fields: old men and women, mothers with their babes tied to
their backs, young lovers who might otherwise have slipped off for a tryst.
Even the fishermen did not go down to their boats for a full two weeks to help with
the stripping, as the harvest was called. Only the littlest boys caught fish in
the shallow waters that ran along the sides of the fields.

So no one saw
the last dragon.

His color was a dull red. Not the red of hollyberry or the red of the flowering trillium, but the red of a man's life-blood spilled out upon the sand. His eyes were black and, when angry, looked as empty as the eyes of a shroud, but when he was calculating they shone with a false jeweled light.
The dragon's tail was long and sinewy, his body longer still. Great mountains rose upon his back. His jaws were a furnace that could roast a whole bull. His wings, still crumpled and weak, lay untested along his sides, but his foreclaws, which had been as brittle as shells at his birth, were now hard as golden oak.

A week later, his wings opened. That night he dreamed of an ocean of blood.

The islands of May and the headland of May's Law — with its hills that the islanders called mountains though they were no more than a shoulder-shrug—lay in the far west of Ingeland. The inhabited islands were named Medd, Marrowbone (because of its shape), Mewl (because the wind made a crying sound across its bird cliffs), St. Marfa's (after the hermit who had lived seventy years in a cave, existing on guano and gulls' eggs), and May's Martyrdom, or just plain Dom.
Few of the Mayers had ever gone inland to the big towns and bigger cities of Ingeland. They had little reason to.

The last town on the biggest island was known as Meddlesome, because in the old days it was where those mettlesome folk who did not get along well with others were sent. Though by this time, they were only a bit quarrelsome with one another. And some of them got along just fine.

It was in this town, where the meat was sweetest because the people were well seasoned, that the last dragon would find its living.

WHERE *IS* THAT GIRL?

SHE ONLY TAKES THAT TONE WITH TANSY.
Tansy
THYme
ELEBY

There were three daughters of a healer who lived on the northern shore of Medd. Although they had proper names after the older gods, they were always called by their herbal names.

Rosemary, the eldest, was a weaver. Dark and not pretty, she had a face that would wear well with time. She had her mother's grey eyes and her passion for work, and wondered that others did not feel the same.

The youngest was the one who was a trouble to her mother.

Early walking, early talking...
...always picking apart anything knit, separating balls of yarn strand by strand...
...always looking for some new herb...
...or shifting things in her father's herb stores, just to see what made them work.
So she was named after the herb that helps women in their time of troubles: Tansy. Her mother hoped she would grow into the name.

Tansy was no color at all. She seemed to blend into her surroundings, whether sparkling by a stream, golden in the sunny meadows...

...shade-colored where the trees overhung the path...

...yellow with a buttercup beneath her chin...

...rosy among the trillium...

...slightly green by the sea.
WHERE *IS* THAT GIRL?

THAT TANSY, LATE AGAIN. PROBABLY DREAMING SOMEWHERE.

SHE HAS KNOWLEDGE, THAT GIRL, AND MORE IMPORTANT-- IMAGINATION.

SHE'S ALREADY AS GOOD A HEALER AS I AM. SOON SHE WILL BE BETTER.

♫ WHEN HE COMES ACROSS THE SEA, HIS LOVING HEART HE'LL GIVE TO ME. ♫

NOW MIND YOU, I'M NOT SAYING SHE DOESN'T HAVE A GIFT. BUT GIFT OR NO, SHE HAS CHORES TO DO. GIFT IS NO EXCUSE. NO EXCUSE AT ALL.

I AM MINDING, MAY-MA.
THWACK

IF SHE WOULD REMEMBER HER CHORES AS WELL AS SHE REMEMBERS THE SEVEN HERBS OF BINDING, THE THREE HERBS FOR SOFT SLEEP, THE NINE HERBS FOR GETTING A WOMAN WITH CHILD...

SHE IS THE DAUGHTER OF A HEALER, MY LOVE. INDEED, SHE *IS* A HEALER. I SHALL FIND HER, NEVER FEAR. AFTER ALL, WHEN I AM GONE, THE VILLAGE WILL HAVE NEED OF HER.

GONE WHERE? ACROSS THE SEA? CAN'T WE SEND SOMEONE TO FIND YOU?
NO, SIMPLETON, HE MEANS WHEN HE IS DEAD.
YOU ARE GOING ***NOWHERE,*** HUSBAND, BUT TO BRING THAT FOOLISH GIRL ***HOME.***

The river was an old one, its bends broad where it flooded at last into the great sea. Here and there the water had cut through soft rock to make islets that could be reached by pole-boat or, in the winter, by walking carefully across the thick ice. Now the turning was green down to the river's edge, and full of cress, reeds, and even wild rice carried from the eastern lands by migrating birds.
RASPBERRIES! WON'T MAY-MA BE PLEASED!

OOH, SOUR. DA WAS RIGHT.
TANSY! TANSY! WHERE ARE YOU, GIRL?
HERE, DA. IN THE RIVER.
WHAT'S THAT? I'VE NEVER SEEN THE LIKES...
WHAT IS IT, DA? I DON'T KNOW IT. IT BURNS SOMETHING FIERCE, THOUGH.
DROP IT! DROP IT AT ONCE, CHILD!
I HAVE NEVER SEEN IT BEFORE, BUT I'VE HEARD OF IT. IT'S CALLED FIREWEED OR FLAMEWORT. I THOUGHT IT WAS BUT A TALE.
AND WHERE WERE YOUR MITTS, GIRL?
I WAS TOO EXCITED TO REMEMBER TO PUT THEM ON.

HERE'S ALOE FOR THE STING...

THE BLISTERS LOOK LIKE SEED PEARLS, DA.
AND TOO PRECIOUS FOR YOUR POOR HANDS, CHILD.

ABOUT FIREWEED. FLAMEWORT. I HAVE JUST REMEMBERED. THE OLD BOOKS SAY IT GROWS ONLY WHERE A GREAT DRAGON LIVES. THERE IS A RHYME...
TELL IT TO ME, DA?

LEAVES OF BLOOD AND SORES OF PEARL, IN THE SEA A SMOKY SWIRL, USE IT FOR YOUR GREATEST NEED, DRAGON'S BANE AND FIREWEED.
DRAGON'S BANE? BUT IF THERE'S BANE, SURELY IT MUST MEAN THERE'S DRAGONS.
NAY, MY SMART GIRL, NO DRAGONS HEREABOUTS FOR HUNDREDS AND HUNDREDS OF YEARS. WHAT USE ARE THESE FLORETS NOW? PERHAPS THEY ARE JUST FOR SHOW.

"IF THE NOTE IN MY OLDEST HERBALRY IS RIGHT, THE WEED WILL BURN FOR NEAR AN HOUR ONCE THE FLORETS OPEN--"
"BURN? LIKE A *FIRE?*"
YOU SAW THE SMOKE IN THE WATER.
THE HERBALRIES FROM THE DRAGON WARS ARE QUITE *SPECIFIC.* AND ALMOST ALWAYS *RIGHT.*
BUT TO ACTUALLY *BURN,* DA...
ALMOST, DA?
WELL, YOU HAVEN'T *SEEN* ANY DRAGONS AROUND HERE, HAVE YOU?

IN ANY CASE, IT BURNS FOR NEAR AN HOUR, THE BOOK SAYS, WITH A STEADY FLAME THAT CANNOT BE PUT OUT. THEN IT CRUMBLES ALL TO ASH. LEAST AS I RECALL IT. WE CAN CHECK LATER.

DO YOU BELIEVE THAT, DA?

NO MORE THAN I BELIEVE THAT DRAGONS ARE STILL AROUND. BUT THOSE PEARLY SORES...

HAVE EITHER OF YOU COME OVER THE SEA?
I CAME BY THE CORACLE DOWN BY THE RIVER--DOES THAT COUNT?
I WILL, IF THAT WILL PLEASE YOU.
IT'S LUCKY YOU'RE SUCH A *CLEVER* GIRL, ROSEMARY.

I AM SHORT OF PEPPERMINT AND SWEET WOODRUFF. WE PASSED SOME DOWN BY THE RIVER. TELL YOUR MA I'LL BE HOME BY DARK.
I WILL, DA.
AND PUT MORE ALOE ON THOSE HANDS.

HMMMM.
QUIET TODAY.
UNNATURAL-LIKE.
WHERE ARE...

...THE BIRDS?

HE'S NEVER LATE, YOUR PA.
HE WAS GOING DOWN TO THE RIVER TO GATHER...
They didn't look for him until near dark. And then, with only their small tapers for light, they missed the herb sack.

The next morning the villagers combed the countryside, but it was Tansy who spotted her father's herb sack lying near the riverbank, a large burn mark along one side.

WHAT CAN THIS MEAN? WHAT COULD HAVE HAPPENED?

COULD DA HAVE BEEN *WRONG* ABOUT THE DRAGON'S BANE?

The books were at best contradictory. Dragon's bane was used to hurt dragons or find dragons or call dragons out. It was a sign dragons were around or that they had all died. It flowered in the spring or the winter or the fall.

ASHES TO ASHES.

WHAT KIND OF FUNERAL IS IT, WITHOUT A BODY? NA-NA, HE WILL BE BACK.
WITHOUT DA, WE SHALL ALL HAVE TO WORK HARDER. OR MARRY WELL. OR BOTH.
THAT BURNED SACK...WHAT DOES IT *MEAN?*

I KNOW YOU ALL MEAN TO COMFORT ME...
DO YOU WANT ME TO GO TO SEA?
DO YOU NEED A MAN AROUND THE HOUSE NOW?

WITHOUT A FATHER, WILL ROSIE FINALLY LISTEN TO MY SUIT?
THE HEALER'S *PROPERTY* IS QUITE FINE. THE WIDOW WILL NEED HELP.

SHE PROBABLY DROVE HIM AWAY WITH HER *NAGGING.*
OH, HE WAS A GOOD MAN.
I WONDER IF SHE WILL SELL THE HERB GARDEN TO ME?

HE'S GONE, MAY-MA.
HE WILL BE BACK. HE WILL.
DEAD, MAY-MA.

HOW COULD HE DO THIS TO ME?

WILL YOU CONSIDER ME NOW, ROSIE? YOUR DA WOULD HAVE WANTED YOU TO BE HAPPY.

SHOULD I SAY ANY-THING? DO I KNOW ENOUGH?

OH, *DA.*

The healer's disappearance became a small mystery in a land used to small mysteries.

But two weeks later, after the harvest was in, Tam the carpenter's finest draft horse, the big grey gelding, was stolen.

Seven days later, two prize ewes were taken from Mother Comfy's fold.

And Meddlesome lived up to its reputation.

YOU ALWAYS FANCIED MY EWES!
I NEVER!

I KNOW IT WAS YOU TOOK ME BEST DRAFT HORSE!
PROVE IT!

DID!
DIDN'T!

YOU'RE A LIAR!
TAKES ONE TO SEE ONE!

MY GOOD PEOPLE...

WHAT ABOUT ME AND MY LOST MAN?!?

THERE MUST BE AN ANSWER IN THE BOOKS. WHAT HAVE I MISSED?

A few days after that, the latest of the cooper's twelve children disappeared from its cradle in the meadow, where the others had left it while they went to pick blaeberries in the dell.
IT'S A RAVENING BEAST!
GOBLINS!
A WERE-WOLF!
HOB-GOBLINS!
VAMPIRES ON THE LOOSE!

MY CHILDREN,
MY CHILDREN, WHO
AMONG YOU HAS EVER
SEEN ANY SUCH
CREATURES?

WHAT AM I TO *DO?* WHAT AM I TO *SAY?*

Still, village life went on: shepherds with their sheep, weavers at the warp, fishermen on the river...

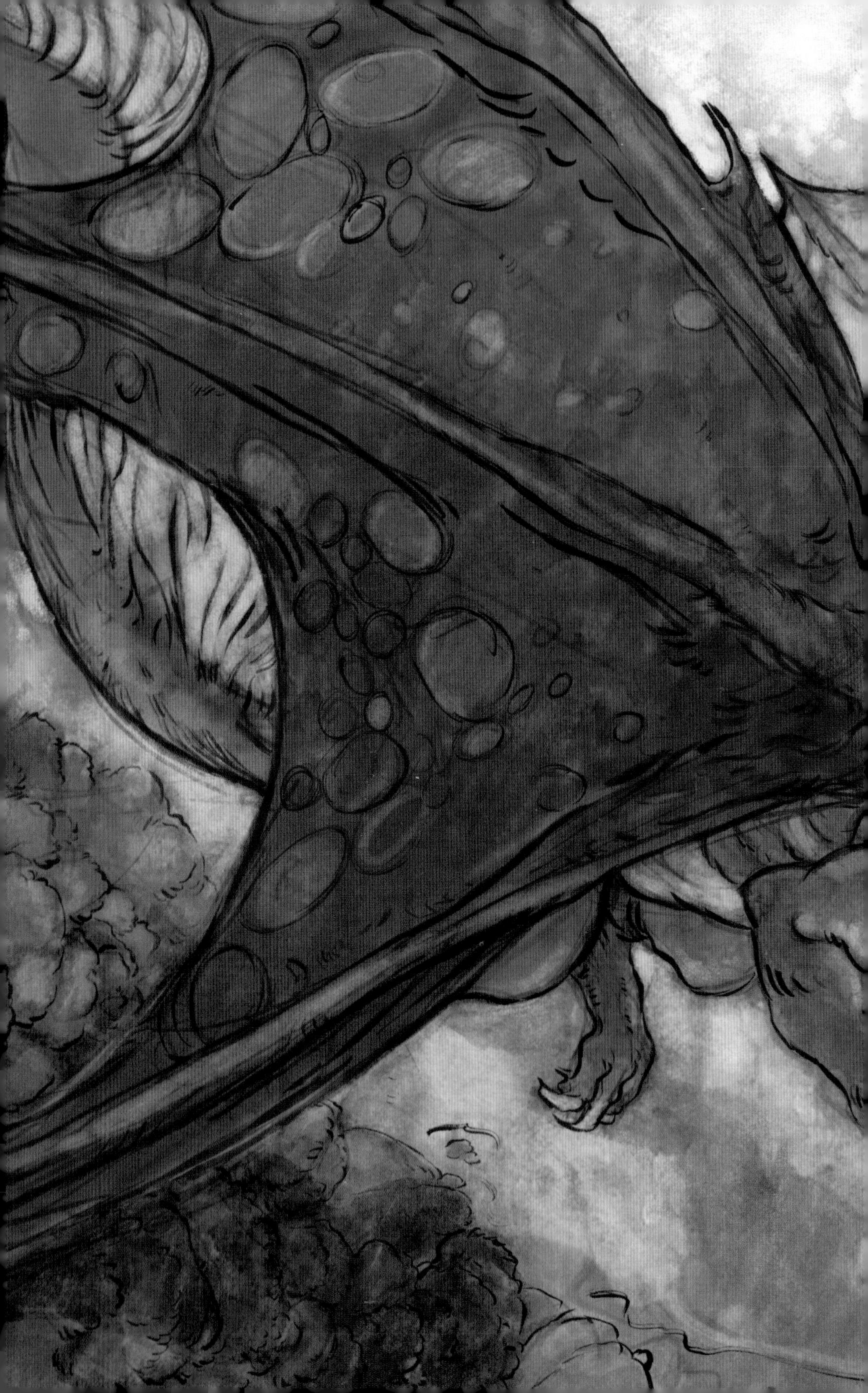

The fisherman stayed in the water and went upriver as far as he could, till the cold drove him out, his hands wrinkled as his grandpap's from their long soaking.

DRAGON!

DRAGON! DRAGON!

No one but Tansy and Rosemary actually believed the fisherman until they saw the broken chain and the bull's blood. Then everyone believed. Even the priest.

As for Tansy—her worst fears were now confirmed. She was certain the entire thing was her fault, as if she had conjured up a dragon from the dragon's bane all on her own.

OH, DA!

HE'S BEEN ET BY THAT DEVIL CREATURE! WHAT NOW, PRIEST?
MA, DOES THAT MEAN BABY WAS ET, TOO?
COOL!

IT COULD HAVE BEEN YOU...
MY GOD, IT COULD HAVE BEEN ME!

DRAGON'S BANE. OF COURSE THERE HAD TO BE A DRAGON.

WE SAY IT EVERY YEAR AT THE PLANTING, THINKING IT MUMMERY. BUT IT'S TRUE, PRIEST. NOW WE KNOW-- IT'S TRUE:
FIRE AND WATER ON THY WING, THE CURSE OF GOD IN BEAK AND FLIGHT!

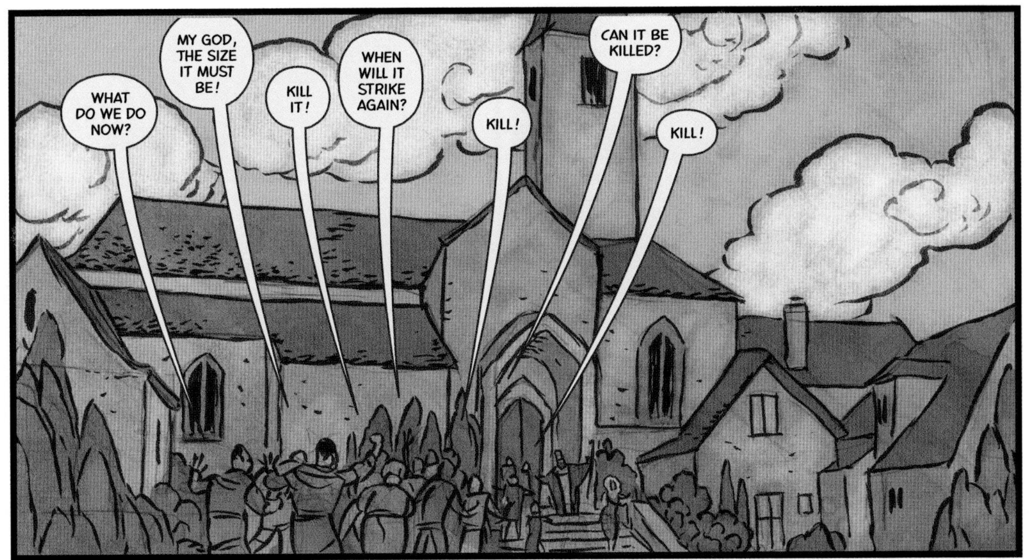
WHAT DO WE DO NOW?
MY GOD, THE SIZE IT MUST BE!
KILL IT!
WHEN WILL IT STRIKE AGAIN?
KILL!
CAN IT BE KILLED?
KILL!

BUT...SURELY DRAGONS DON'T HAVE BEAKS.

I DON'T KNOW. DON'T BLASPHEME, GOOD PEOPLE. I...
...I...DON'T KNOW.
I MAY HAVE ANSWERS. I HAVE A BOOK...

IT'S BEEN IN MY FAMILY FOR GENERATIONS...
...AND IT'S ALL ABOUT DRAGONS.

THE OLD COOT! HE ALWAYS HAS A BOOK.
MUCH GOOD IT DOES HIM!

SHOW ME.

I ***MUST*** SEE WHAT'S IN THAT BOOK. IT MAY BE THE KEY.

THIS IS THE IMPORTANT PART...

"YE EATING HABITS OF AN FULLY FLEDGED DRACONIS..."

A fully fledged draconis will suppe and digeste an infant in a daye, often supplementing the small meal with birds.

It will suppe and digeste a grown man or woman in five dayes, though if the man or woman be large and of a meaty composition, ye draconis may take an extra halfe daye before it needs to feed again.

...este an ewe i...
...es an owle, t...
...been shorne...

...ppe and digeste...
...es, a large heav...

full grown bull or bullock ye draconis will
and digeste in fourteen dayes, being logie
rific for several dayes after first it eats.
o dayes,
eece if the
alle horse in
ttle horse in

WE CAN KILL IT WHILE IT SLEEPS OFF ITS MEAL.
THERE ARE OLD ARROWS IN THE TOWN HALL, FROM THE DRAGON WARS.
BUT HOW CAN WE KNOW WHERE IT LIES?

AND HOW DO WE KNOW THIS INFORMATION IS CORRECT?
DRAGONS CAN BREATHE FIRE, YOU KNOW.
MY BABY...

IF THE BOOK IS RIGHT, WE HAVE TWO WEEKS BEFORE...

...BEFORE THE DRAGON FEEDS AGAIN.

WHAT CAN A GIRL KNOW ABOUT SUCH THINGS?
THIS IS MEN'S WORK!

WELL, SHE CAN READ.

SHE'S THE HEALER'S DAUGHTER, NOT SOME COMMON GIRL.

SHE'S THE HEALER NOW.

The villagers put aside their differences—at least for a while—settling into the more important work of making, mustering, and mastering the old weapons.

It had been years—generations, really—since the anvils had been used for making other than shovels or harrows, plows or rakes. Now what was needed were pikes with fierce points and swords with sharp edges.

YOU HAVE ALREADY DONE ENOUGH, WARNING US.
IF I CAN'T KEEP YOU SAFE, ROSIE, WHAT KIND OF MAN AM I?

WE ARE FARMERS AND FISHERMEN, BEEKEEPERS AND SMITHS. WE CANNOT DEFEAT A DRAGON BY OURSELVES.

WE NEED...

WE NEED A *DRAGON-SLAYER.*

Yes, a dragonslayer—and before the dragon roused from its stupor. Two weeks the book said, two weeks after eating a bull. But where did one look for a hero? A dragonslayer? It had been centuries since the dragon wars.

Finally, three boys were sent to search for a dragonslayer, if only to keep them safe and away from the village: the cooper's outspoken son, the son of the smith, and the fisherman's younger brother, whom he'd raised since their mother had died in childbirth.

BLESS YOU, BOYS, AND MAY GOD'S HAND KEEP YOU SAFE.

DO NOT TARRY. WE HAVE BARELY TWELVE DAYS NOW.

BONG
BONG
BONG

As the boys left, the sexton rang Great Tom, the treble bell that had been cast in the hundredth year after the victory over the dragons. On its side was the inscription: *I am Tom, when I toll there is fire, when I thunder, there is victory.*

Netherdale
Mortend
Severance
Yetts of Marrow
Barleybyre
Milton of Sandhurl
Swinekin
Merle
Tarleton
Trinn
Meddlesome
The boys landed on the mainland at Swinekin. Not the worst town in the realm, but certainly filled with its share of flea-infested villains, all more interested in raising a pint of ale than raising a crop of corn.
There, the boys found "heroes" aplenty.

OF COURSE I'M A HERO! I CAN OUTDRINK ANY MAN HERE, OVER OR UNDER THE TABLE.

SO CAN MY FATHER. AND HE'S NO HERO.

NEVER MIND. WE'RE SURE TO FIND A REAL HERO SOON.
ELEVEN DAYS.
THAT'S FIVE DAYS THERE AND SIX TO GET BACK HOME.

THIS LAUREL CROWN WAS FOR HEROISM IN THE MIDST OF BATTLE.

WOULD THAT I COULD, BOYS, BUT THE ONLY BATTLES I CAN FIGHT THESE DAYS ARE THE ONES IN MY *DREAMS.*

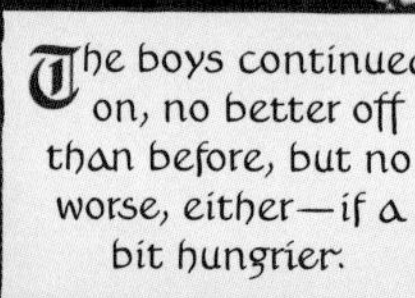
The boys continued on, no better off than before, but no worse, either—if a bit hungrier.

HEY-- LOOK OVER THERE!

IF *HE'S* NOT A HERO, THEN I'M A *PORK PIE!*

HEY, YOU-- SIR!

WELL, A MEAT-HEAD, AT LEAST!

PARDON ME, MA'AM--WE'RE LOOKING FOR A HERO.

WOULD A SHERO DO?

ALONE WITH THREE BOYS ON THE ROAD? NOT IF YOU WANT A WEDDING, GIRL!

PAAAAAAA!

TOO BAD...
NINE DAYS LEFT-- THREE HERE, SIX TO GET HOME.
FOUR DAYS HERE AND FIVE BACK--IF WE RUN.

They found more heroes than they could use—

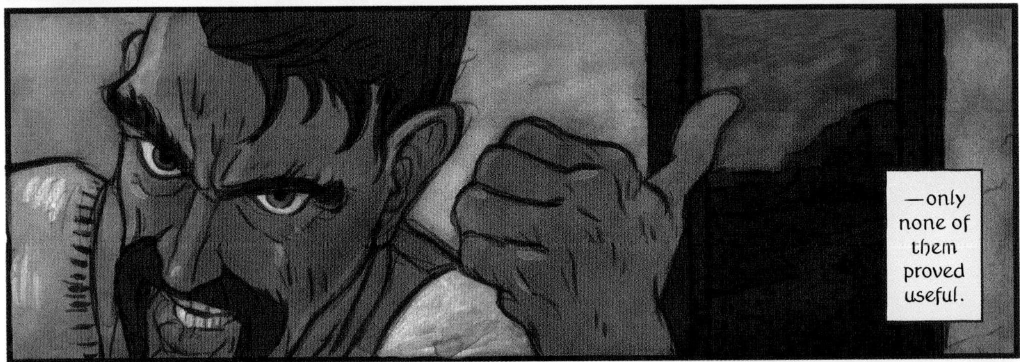
—only none of them proved useful.

And then, in a tosspot inn in the town of Netherdale, on the very last day before they had to return home, they found him.

They knew him for a hero the moment he stood.

HE CERTAINLY LOOKS LIKE A HERO!
DID YOU SEE THOSE MUSCLES? EVEN BIGGER THAN THAT FARM GIRL'S!
SO WHY IS HE HERE, IN THIS TOSSPOT INN?
HE'S DRINKING, YOU IDJIT. HEROES DO THAT.

BE YOU A HERO?

THERE'S MONEY TO BE MADE HERE.

FEEL THAT ARM!
LIKE IRON!

WOW!
HOW DO YOU DO THAT?
WHY DO YOU DO THAT?

NOW THAT'S AWESOME.
HERO OR NO HERO, THAT'S ME GOOD POKER!

HE'S LIKE A HERO RIGHT OUT OF THE STORIES!
HE COULD STRANGLE THE WYRM WITH ONE HAND!

WHAT'S YOUR NAME, SIR?

MY NAME IS LANCOT, SON.
A HERO'S NAME!

BUT WHY IS HE *HERE,* IN THIS DRUNKARD'S DREAM?

The boys shared their pennies and bought Lancot a mug of stew and many mugs of ale. He remembered things for them then. Service to a faerie queen. A battle with a walking tree.
Giants slain in five different shires.
Three goblins spitted on his sword...
...WHICH LEFT IT SO PITTED BY GOBLIN BLOOD, I BURIED IT WITH THEM IN A COMMON GRAVE!
His stories grew with the night, and they doled out their coins in exchange. Each thought it a good bargain.

SLEEP WELL, LADS.
HEROES ARE THIN ON THE GROUND THESE DAYS--
--AT LEAST NOW YOU CAN GO HOME WITH A BUNCH OF FINE TALES.

YAWN
OOOOOHH, MY HEAD...

INKEEP, CAN WE HAVE SOME BREAKF--
--HEY!
WHERE'S LANCOT?
THAT TOSSPOT? PROBABLY LONG ON HIS WAY.

They ran after him. He was their best real hope for a hero. He was their *only* real hope. And time was running out.

HOI! HERO!

WE HAVE A PROPOSITION FOR YOU--
--A HERO'S JOB.

THERE'S GOLD IN IT.
WHAT GOLD?
SHUT UP.

GOLD?

WE'D BUY YOU BREAKFAST, LANCOT, BUT WE'VE...*ER*...RUN THROUGH ALL OUR MONEY.
PERHAPS ***YOU*** COULD PAY FOR IT?
AS LONG AS I AM PAID BACK ONCE WE REACH YOUR ISLE. WITH INTEREST.

WHAT'S INTEREST?
THIS IS NEVER GOING TO WORK!

They feasted their way back home, hardly worrying about time. They had their hero, after all, so what did they care?

Meanwhile in Meddlesome, everyone worked together to make their village dragon-proof—as if such a thing were possible.
NOW DON'T YE GO CRYIN' TO YER MA OVER EVERY LITTLE CUT.
READY WITH MORE NETTING, LADIES?
THE FOOD IS IN CASE OF A DRAGON SIEGE.
STARVING US OUT.
WHAT'S A SIEGE, MA?

Otherwise, life went on much as it always had.
I WOULD RATHER DIE WITH YOU THAN BE WITHOUT YOU.

THEN I SHALL HAVE TO TEACH YOU TO BAIT A HOOK.
PERHAPS I SHALL DIE INSTEAD.

NONE OF YOU COMES FROM OVER THE SEA. LEAVE ME BE--

"--JUST GO AND KILL THAT DRAGON!"

"Fourteen days," the book said, but how accurate that might be, no one knew, nor whether the dragon would be roused by anything but hunger.
CLANG
CLANG
CLANG

The bell was discovered in the ruins.
The sexton, poor man, was never found.

WHY IS
IT SO QUIET?
I NEVER SAW
A VILLAGE SO
QUIET.

MAYBE
THEY'RE ALL
ASLEEP.

IT'S THREE
BY THE SUN.
WHAT SAYS
THE BELL?
WHERE
IS THE
BELL?

AND THE
TOWER?

SO THERE WENT THE SEXTON, HOLDING ON TO THE ROPE--
--IN THE AIR, HE WENT--
--AND THE DRAGON, IT WAS HUGE! FLOWN BACK OVER THE SEA--
DRAGON? DRAGON?!

NO ONE SAID ANYTHING TO ME ABOUT A DRAGON!
WHAT AN INTERESTING-LOOKING MAN! PERHAPS HE'S COME ACROSS THE OCEAN FOR ME.

STRONG ENOUGH. BUT IS HE WILLING TO WORK?

POOR MAN. HE'S NO HERO AT ALL.

As there was no inn in the village, May-ma had the best claim upon the hero. After all, it was her husband who had been the dragon's first victim.
They clamored for stories of his adventures. But in this place of real dragons, what stories could he tell?

WE'RE COUNTING ON YOU TO KILL THAT HORRIBLE BEAST.

I EXPECT IT WON'T BE EASY.

DID YOU COME FROM ACROSS THE SEA?

WE HAVE DRAGON'S BANE...
DRAGON'S *WHAT?*

DA KNEW. THOUGH HE BELIEVED IT MEANT NAUGHT.

AND LOOK WHERE HIS *NAUGHT* GOT HIM.

IT GOT HIM *ET.*
WHEN WERE YOU PLANNING TO TELL US, TANSY?

I DIDN'T WANT TO SAY ANYTHING UNTIL I WAS CERTAIN, ELSE I'D HAVE GIVEN FALSE HOPE TO THE VILLAGE.

WELL, WE HAVE *NO* HOPE NOW, BECAUSE THE DRAGON IS HERE. AND NOW I'LL NEVER MEET MY TRUE LOVE, BECAUSE I'LL BE *ET* FIRST!

AHEM.
WHAT EXACTLY DOES DRAGON'S BANE *DO?*

WELL, A BANE IS...

IF YOU KNOW HOW TO WORK WITH IT...

KEEPS YOU FROM GETTING ET, I GUESS...

THE BANE GROWS WHERE THERE ARE DRAGONS. AND IT CAN COMBUST.

COMBUST-- THAT'S GOOD, ISN'T IT?

SO, WHAT DO YOU LIKE TO DO--BESIDES BEING A ***HERO?***

WHAT CAN I TELL THEM? PLAYING AT HERO IS ALL I'VE DONE SINCE I WAS FIFTEEN. TEN YEARS.

AS A BOY, ROSEMARY MEANS. BEFORE YOU WERE A HERO.

AS A BOY? I LIKED...TO FLY KITES, I SUPPOSE.

USELESS WASTE OF STICKS AND STRING!

BUT LITTLE WORMS ARE USEFUL FOR TURNING THE SOIL TO MAKE HERBS GROW. IT IS THE GREAT WYRMS THAT ARE OUR ENEMIES.
BUT IN THE END, THEY ALL ET US UP.
AND WHAT DO *KITES* HAVE TO DO WITH ANY OF THIS?
AHEM. THANKS FOR DINNER, LADIES. IT'S BEEN A LONG WALK TO MEDDLE-SOME, AND SOME LONG DAYS STILL AHEAD. I'M FOR BED.

In the morning, the villagers arrived, looking for their hero.

IS HE UP?
I'LL WAKE HIM. THOUGH WHY HE'S ASLEEP AT THIS HOUR, WHEN ALL GOOD PEOPLE ARE ABOUT THEIR WORK...

ROSIE...HAVE I ASKED SOME-THING WRONG?

IT'S THE HERO. HE'S A LAYABOUT AND A...KITE FLIER. HIS CHARM IS A MILE WIDE AND AN INCH DEEP. I HAVE NO IDEA WHY THEY HAVE BROUGHT HIM HERE.

KITE FLIER?
DO NOT ASK.

GO, WOMAN! LET ME GET DRESSED. TELL THEM I'LL BE THERE ANON.

IS THERE A BACK DOOR?

DO WE START TODAY?
SWORDS OR SPEARS?
WE'VE GOT GAFF HOOKS!

NOW, LADS, SLAYING A DRAGON NEEDS A SOLID PLAN.
COME BACK TOMORROW, AND I WILL HAVE A PLAN TO SHARE WITH YOU.

BETTER YET--THE DAY AFTER TOMORROW.
BEGGING YOUR PARDON, BUT THE DAY AFTER TOMORROW MAY BE TOO LATE. WHAT IF THE GREAT WYRM RETURNS TO FEED? THE SEXTON WAS A...A PUNY MAN.

TILL TOMORROW, THEN--AND THE PLAN!

THERE YOU ARE!

OOPS-- WRONG WAY.

BEING A HERO DOES NOT MEAN YOU ARE WITHOUT FEAR. ONLY FOOLS LACK FEAR. I KNOW YOU ARE NO FOOL.
NO. NO FOOL. NO ***HERO,*** EITHER.

I AM NO HERO, EITHER. TO RUN AWAY IS THE MOST SENSIBLE THING EITHER OF US COULD DO. BUT THAT WON'T STOP THE GREAT WYRM FROM DEVOURING EVERYONE IN MY VILLAGE--AND, ULTIMATELY, ALL OF INGELAND.

YOU MENTIONED KITES. I THOUGHT THEY MIGHT BE PART OF YOUR PLAN.
I MET A MAGE ONCE, WITH STRANGE HIGH CHEEKBONES. HE SPOKE WITH AN ACCENT THAT JANGLED THE EAR. HE TOLD ME IN HIS TONGUE, THE WORD FOR KITE IS *DRACHE*, DRAGON.

YES! HEALERS KNOW THIS BY THE NAME *CORRESPONDENCE*. IT IS THE FIRST RULE OF HERBALRY.
LIKE CALLS TO LIKE. LIKE DRAWS OUT LIKE.

AND I FOUND THE PERFECT STICKS FOR A KITE.
LIKE CALLS TO LIKE, EH?

THE PAPER IS FROM MAY-MA--A RECIPE FOR MULBERRY WINE.
I THOUGHT-- ***YOUR*** PLAN...

--AND USE IT TO DELIVER A KILLING BLOW!

OF COURSE! BUT--AH--THE *KILLING* BLOW--

--SURELY YOU DON'T MEAN TO FLY ME UP ON THE KITE TO DO BATTLE?
YOU ARE NO HERO. AND I AM NO KITE HANDLER.

YOU WILL NOT GO UP ON THE KITE. I FORBID IT.
I AM NOT YOURS TO FORBID.
BESIDES, WHAT I HAVE IN MIND IS SOMETHING QUITE DIFFERENT.

As the river rilled over the rocks to the sea, Tansy spelled out her plan. It had been born when Lancot first mentioned kites, and it would take the entire village. There were to be no heroes, only hard work.
I WILL NEED PAINT--RED AS BLOOD AND BLACK AS HOPE.
IS HOPE NOT A LIGHTER COLOR?
NOT WHEN DEALING WITH DRAGONS.

The cooper supplied both buckets and paint.
The leftover nappies of the missing babe, the petticoats of six village maidens, the healer's favorite shirt, and Sage's prettiest ribbands were torn up for binding.
Four huge, precious books of church receipts were torn apart for the paper.
Boys were sent to fetch lumber from the woods.
AS THE DRAGON IS MIGHTY, YET CAN SAIL THROUGH THE AIR WITHOUT FALLING, SO MUST THE WOOD OF OUR *DRACHE* LIKEWISE BE STRONG YET LIGHT.

HE'S AWFULLY ODD, FOR A HERO.
I THOUGHT HE'D GO AFTER THE DRAGON WITH A SWORD.
OR A LANCE.
OR A PIKE.
BUT A KITE? THAT'S COOL.

There was an atmosphere of a pleasure fair in the village. But boys were stationed at the outskirts of Meddlesome to watch the skies, and every door in the village lay open wide for a quick escape indoors.
Lancot showed the villagers how to soak the wood in water to make it flex, and how to bind the flexed and rounded wood with rags.
Rosemary turned out to be the best at making the hoops, proud how well her nimble fingers could work.
HERE ARE SOME STAVES YOU CAN USE AS WELL.
I HOPE THIS IS NOT A WASTE OF GOOD CLOTH.
OH, HUSH. IT WILL BE NO WASTE IF IT HELPS TO KILL THAT MURDERING WYRM!

The villagers made rounded hoops, the largest twice as big as a man, then descending in size. The middle link's circumference was that of Great Tom's bow, and the last was the size of the priest's dinner plate.
Tansy plaited rope of trailing vines, horsehair, fisherman's hemp, and a bit of her own locks. She whispered a charm as she worked.
MAY BONE UPON BONE SAFELY FIT AND THIS MAN'S BONES BE NOT UNKNIT.
WELL DONE, ALL. WE ARE NEAR FINISHED.

SOON I MUST DO MY PART--

With every man, woman, and child holding a hoop, they marched the great *drache* from the village to the shore.

SEE HOW BRAVE LANCOT IS--NEVER ONCE LOOKING TO THE SKY!
WOW!

OF COURSE HE NEVER LOOKS AT THE SKY, FOR THAT'S WHERE HIS DREAD LIES.

FLY WITH THE HOPES OF MEN TO GUIDE YOU, FLY WITH THE HEART OF A HERO TO GOAD YOU...
FLY WITH THE SPIRIT OF GOD TO GUARD YOU, BLESSINGS TO YOU, BEAK AND TAIL.
A FINE SLATE ON WHICH TO SCRIPT OUR CHALLENGE TO THE WYRM!
NOW...

...LET'S GET THIS *DRACHE* INTO THE AIR!

The wind fretted and goaded the kite, and the links began to swim through the air, faster, higher.
I'M FLYING! FLYING!
DROP, AMBER-ROSE, AND I WILL CATCH YOU!
MAKE HER FAST, MEN. THAT TREE IS THE LARGEST ALONG THE RIVER. IT SHOULD DO WHAT WE CANNOT: HOLD THE KITE WHEN THE DRAGON COMES.
NOW, RUN BACK HOME. STICK TO THE TREES, AND HURRY. THE DRAGON COULD BE HERE WITHIN THE HOUR.
TANSY AND I WILL FINISH HERE.

THE NEXT WORK IS MINE, HERO.
TIME FOR YOU TO LEAVE, TOO.
NO. I'M ***NOT*** LEAVING.

I WOULD NOT HAVE YOU FALL IN.
THAT'S ALL RIGHT. I CAN SWIM.
GOOD. *I* CAN'T.

FIREWEED WILL BURN ONLY FLESH, NOT CLOTH. AND DRAGONS ARE FLESH, UNDER A COAT OF MAIL.
THAT'S DRAGON'S BANE? THAT PRETTY BOUQUET?

CAREFUL. THE FLORETS--

OW!
I THGGT YOO WRR JKNNG!

I'LL GET THE ALOE FROM MY BAG--IT WILL SOOTHE YOUR HAND.

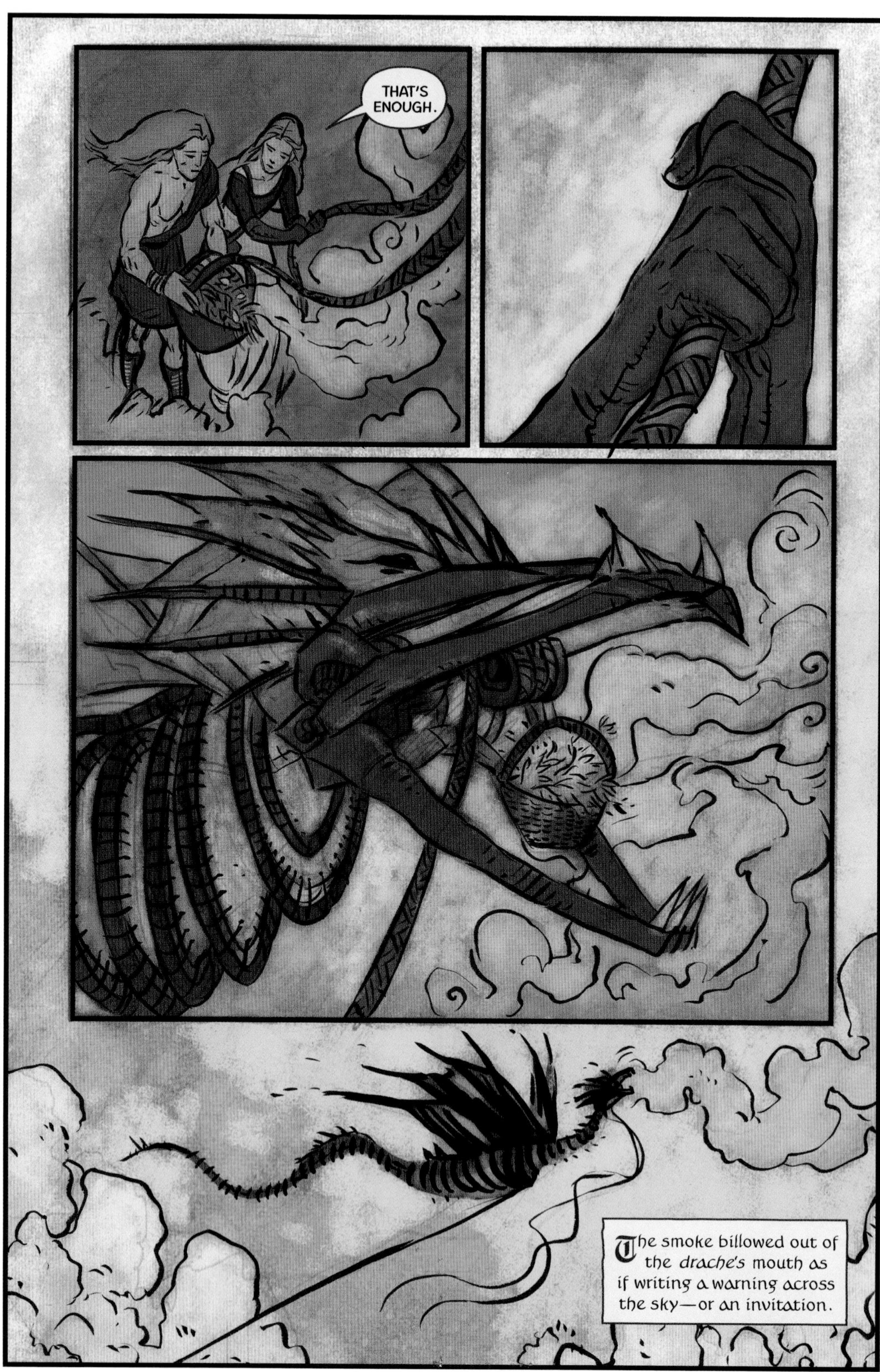
THAT'S ENOUGH.
The smoke billowed out of the *drache's* mouth as if writing a warning across the sky—or an invitation.

NOW WE FIND COVER AND WAIT.

I WONDER HOW LONG IT WILL BE.

GET DOWN! AND HUSH!

VERMIFAX MAJOR...OH, GOD, THE SMELL!
COUGH COUGH

SMACK

I'M SORRY! DID I HURT YOU?
HUSH, YOU DID THE RIGHT THING. IT WAS ONLY A SMALL PAIN, BUT IF THE BEAST HAD HEARD ME AND HURT YOU...

I... YOU...

TIME ENOUGH FOR THAT WHEN THE DRAGON IS DEAD.

COURTING?
MORE LIKE A MANLY CHALLENGE.

SNAP

IT'S *GONE.* THE BASKET WITH THE BANE IS...
GONE.

WHERE ARE YOU GOING?
TO GET MORE BANE.
IS THERE ANY LEFT?

OW!
OW!
OW!

I HAVE GATHERED ALL THERE IS. NOT A LOT.
NO, USE THE MITTS FROM MY POCKET.

WHY DID *YOU* NOT WEAR THEM?
I WAS IN TOO MUCH OF A HURRY.

AND HOW DO I GET THESE UP TO THE DRAGON?
I'VE GOT A PLAN.

I'VE GOT A PLAN. YOUR HANDS ARE TOO BURNED.

YOU STAY HERE AND PUT SOME HALLOW ON THOSE PALMS.
ALOE.
THAT, TOO.

LANCOT...
I...YOU...
GODSPEED.
As he climbed, Lancot could feel his heart hammering. The skin on the back of his neck and shoulders rippled with fear. He could hear the wind whistling past his bared teeth, could feel tears teasing from his eyes.

The dragon attacked the kite full force, raging at its enemy.

I DON'T DARE LOOK DOWN.

LOOK AT ME, YOU MISBEGOTTEN BEAST!
IT'S DINNER-TIME!

OPEN YOUR DAMNED MOUTH!

PERFECT!

The great dragon began to burn from the inside out. Even from where she stood, Tansy could see the red aureole around its body and flames flickering from its mouth to its tail. It turned slowly in the air as if each movement brought pain.

LANCOT!

VRAAAAM
NOT THE WATER... NO!!

The gulls were unaccountably silent. From behind her, an owl called its place from tree to tree. A small breeze teased into the willows. Hearing a bigger sound nearby, Tansy shrank into herself, even though she knew the dragon was absolutely and irretrievably dead.

BUT YOU CAN'T SWIM!
TURNS OUT IT'S A LOW TIDE. AND I CAN *WADE.*

There is a large mount of ash-colored rock that appears and disappears as the tide ebbs and flows. No birds ever land there, and seals avoid it as well. The May islanders call the place "Wyrm's Head," and once a year they row out to picnic on the islet and fly their kites.

A great dragon kite, known as the Hero Kite, always sails high above the rest.

Just at dusk, the village storyteller and innkeeper—Lancot—sets the dragon kite on fire. When the kite is fully aflame, he lets the rope go and the kite flies off into the prevailing winds and out to sea, the ash tumbling down into the water, and disappearing below the waves.
SOME DAY, I SHALL HAVE TO TEACH YOU TO SWIM.
IT'S NOT NECESSARY, MY LOVE. AFTER ALL--I CAN WADE.

The End